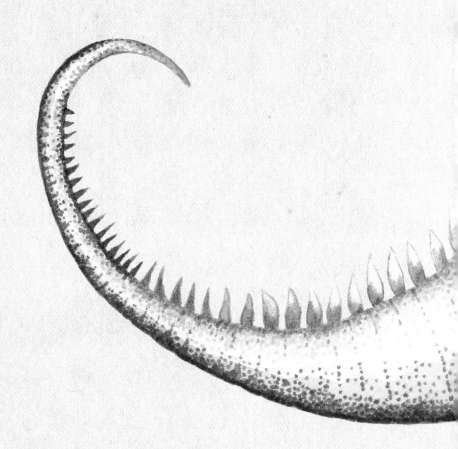

to: Ari~
Poetry is fun. Imagination...awesome!
. 2019.
Jayne M. Rose-Vallee

Dinosaurs Living in MY HAIR! 2

by Jayne M. Rose-Vallee

illustrated by Anni Matsick

These curls disrupt my first grade life,
they're messy and "not cool."
Mean kids in class make fun of me,
they tease, and ridicule.

And last year three small dinosaurs
moved in *my* hair to play.
I worried they would drive me nuts,
but it's turned out okay.

Some dinosaurs? Impossible!
I'm telling you it's true.
If you look close, T-Rex is here
and near *my* bow are two.

I have four friends in my classroom
who share a common trait.
Espuardo, Faye, Chanelle and Gage
have hair that won't stay straight.

That's Billy Cline who torments us.
He stuffed Faye's hat with dirt.
He put some glue in Gage's curls,
and called Espuardo "Twerp."

To make it worse, Mike E. sits here.
He hides things in *my* hair,
like paper wads, and pencil parts,
and chewed gum when he's dared.

He calls me names if I complain
no matter what I do.
"Frizz Head," "Mop Top," "Wil-de-beest,"
are only just a few.

I write *my* name in big bold print
and hold it up to him.
"It's S – A – B – R – I – N – A;
don't call me names again!"

He smirks at me and I stare back
and then we hear "RECESS!"

I join my friends up on the bars.
We flip, our curls a mess.

Then all at once, I feel a yank
and hear a whooshing sound.
One dinosaur has lost its grip
and fallen to the ground!

I am in shock. I gasp, afraid.
What will *my* four friends say?
And then I see Chanelle *jump* down
and whisper, "Hey, no way!"

"You've got dinos? That's so cool!"
Espuardo says, "Me too!"
"Me three," says Gage. "I've got some. Look!"
And then I see it's true.

We do not hear the recess bell.
We do hear Mike E. shout.
"Hey, Noodle Heads, the bell just rang."
T-Rex says, "Tune him out!"

I feel him there in back of me.
(He likes to come in last.)
That's when he puts a beetle in
my curls, it happens FAST!

The T-Rex slurps the beetle up
and nips at Mike E.'s skin.
Mike hollers, "Ouch!" in disbelief
and I begin to grin.

And just like that, T-Rex is gone.
He hides without a trace.
I tell Mike E. "STOP. BUGGING. ME!"
I hope I've made my case.

Mike E. then finds an old gum drop
and throws it at my head.
Velociraptor swings her tail
and smacks it out instead!

Velociraptor and T-Rex,
together with Bronto,
stick out their heads while we join in:
"You bullies have to go!"

As days go on, the dinosaurs
teach us some things to try:
make eye contact, stand up straight,
be gutsy versus shy.

We toss mean words into the trash
and tell adults at school.
It's never wrong to walk away.
Be confident and cool.

You might think that the dinosaurs
were key to our success,
but friends and self-acceptance are
the answer I profess.

I can't believe it's really true
our hair now brings us fun!
My friends and I create a force –
all different, and yet one!

Dinosaurs Living in MY HAIR! 2
Published by Rosevallee Creations LLC

ROSEVALLEE
CREATIONS

First Edition 2018
ISBN 978-0-9861922-2-7

Join the DLIMH Movement!

Visit our website http://DinosaursLivinginMyHair.com
http://RoseValleeCreations.com

• Purchase fun DLIMH accessories.
• Invite author Jayne M. Rose-Vallee to read at your school.
• Stay up to date on new dinosaur discoveries.
• Find out where DLIMH will be next.

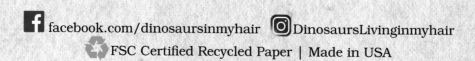

facebook.com/dinosaursinmyhair DinosaursLivinginmyhair

FSC Certified Recycled Paper | Made in USA